NEIL PASRICHA

AWESOME

IS EVERYWHERE

ARE YOU READY?

Tap the Earth...

Good job!
Tap it again...

We're getting closer.
We're going in.
One more time?

Wow!

The waves are beating the sandy shore.

Tilt the book away from you and give it a shake.

Feel the hot sunbeams on your skin.
Hear the wind whispering through the tall palm trees in the distance.

Take a deep breath and sniff the warm, wet, salty air...
Try blowing on the waves ... just a little bit...

Hmmm...
Try blowing harder — as hard as you can!

Whoa!
Quick—take a deep breath and flip
the book over your head!

Doesn't everything sound quieter down here?
It's a private and peaceful place in the world.
Keep holding your breath.
Stop and listen to your heartbeat.

Now let your breath out and
bring the book back down ...
slowly.

Feel the warm sun on your face.
Feel your body getting a little lift as the waves roll past.
The warm water rushes over your toes and ankles and legs.
Reach out and tap the sand...

There are millions of sand grains right in front of you.
The Earth is made of sand.
There is sand under the houses, roads, and lakes of the world.
Rub your hand and feel the sand give
you a million little massages.
Now tap the sand again.

Wow!
It's incredible to see all the detail in the world.
Every single thing is made up of smaller and smaller things!

Now ... shake the book and see what happens.

Good job!
Now give it an even bigger shake.
The biggest shake you can!
How far out can we fly?

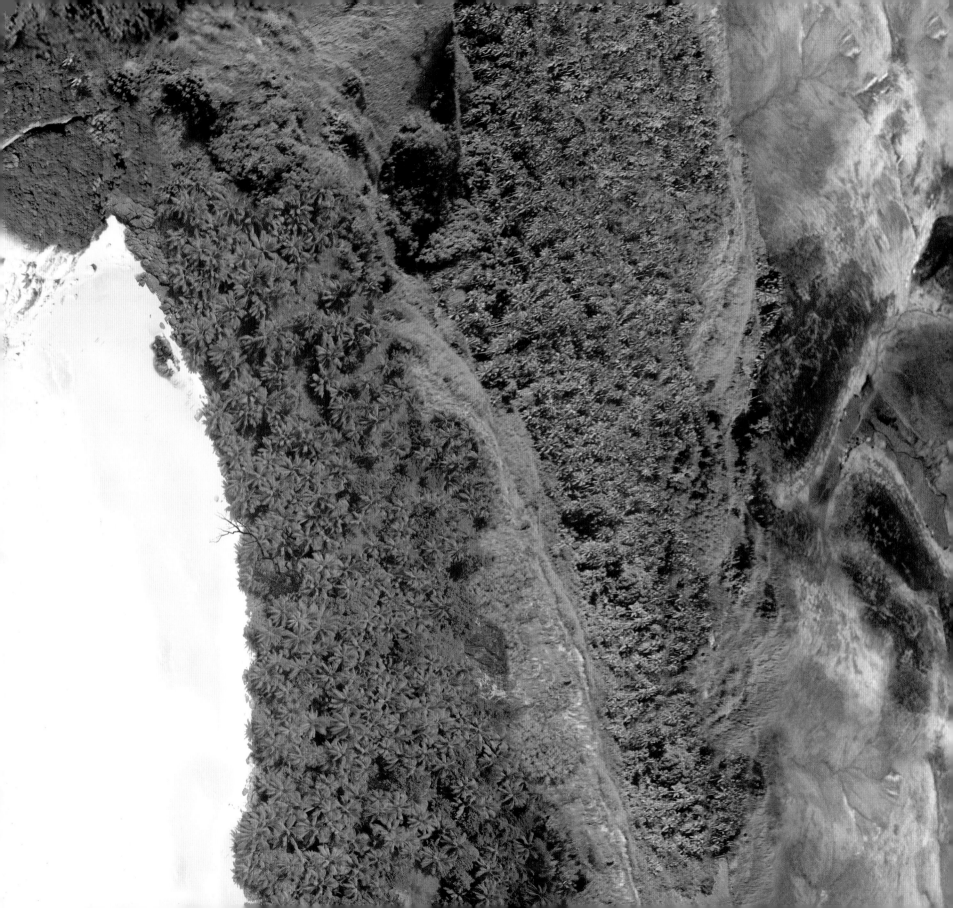

Wow!
We zoomed in and zoomed all the way out again.
We can fly our minds to anywhere on Earth...
We can fly through clouds...
Jump in waves...
Lie on sand...

Awesome is everywhere.

But you know where the best place of all is?

HERE.